This is Your Life

A Road to Healing

W. James Harris

This is Your Life

A Road to Healing

W. James Harris

Copyright © 2011 W. James Harris

All rights reserved.

ISBN: 0983577110

ISBN-13: 9780983577119

Published by: Harris-Moore Publishing

This is Your Life

A Road to Healing

W. James Harris

Publisher

Baltimore, Maryland

Dedication

To My Lovely wife, my angel Cheryl who laid the foundation for the man that I am today, who gave her life that I may live. I am eternally grateful. To my devoted friend and partner, Zina (Ms. Z) who filled the gap and helped me build the bridge to my destiny. And to my children, biological and spiritual, my family and friends I thank you, especially those that believe that I am what I am.

Foreward

The book or I should say the writing; **"This Is Your Life"** is just that, your life, told from the author's point of view. In many ways he cleverly uses his wit to describe a journey he took through life to give the illusion it was just his life. However, if you take a closer look at the story you'll start to discover how the events in his life are really a parallel in how every day life unfolds compared to your own. As we Journey through a space and time called life the wisdom and knowledge one potentially gains is immeasurable. **"This is Your Life"** is a fictional account of one man's Journey but parallels the real life journey of many. As you walk the path through the unimaginable memories of a man that learned by trial and error, envision your own Journey. What steps did you take to get to where you are today? What catastrophic event completely altered your life and how you viewed living? What kept you on the road continuing down an unknown path headed for a certain destiny, discovering who and what you really are.

Table Of Contents

Prologue

DENISE'S DEATH

On August, 20th, 2006 a cloud came over me blocking the sun's rays, on December 20th that warm reflected glow turn black, but it was impossible for me to even notice because I was wearing the darkest pair of sun shades known to man.

Who I'm I, the person next door, your friend, a total stranger, but most of all I'm you.

Let's rewind this story back to 30 something years before when I was a young impressionable lad. Coming out of the sixties, where slogans like *"Peace, Love, Rock and Roll"; "Give Peace a Chance"; "I Have a Dream"; "Ask Not What Your Country Can do for You, But What You Can do for Your Country"*; it was easy to think the world was changing. So I did what every misguided young man would do, I joined the war!

CHAPTER 1

THE NAVY

For me the war was the Navy, you know sail the seven seas and see the world.

Mind you up to now my world was this little town with a thousand stories, and this is just one of them.

Looking back over that period in my life I've come to the conclusion I wouldn't change a thing.

I'm pretty sure I would have followed the exact same path, except this time, I wouldn't talk as much, as the old saying goes, silence is golden.

Why did I choose the Navy as a way out of my little town, well that's a million dollar question, but one simple answer, I wanted out.

As a little boy I remember passing this poster sitting beside our house with a picture of a sailor in his "Navy Whites".

There was something about that white flap trimmed in blue and those wide legged bell bottoms.

I remember wondering what could be the purpose of having thirteen buttons across the front of your pants.

At the time I had little if any knowledge of the first thirteen colonies forming the first union we now call the United States.

When we think of these United States the truth sometimes escapes us about how it started with only thirteen states, never the less the poster intrigued me.

On the poster the words "Join the Navy" and "See the World" was placed ever so careful in big bold letters across the top of the image.

Slung over his right shoulder was his life, a big green *Duffle bag.*

This *Duffle bag* he carried must have been full of mysteries because the look in his eyes led me to believe he was on a mission.

I wanted that life, at least that's what I thought at the tender age of seventeen.

The image on the poster drew me to the Navy like a moth is drawn to a flame.

It seemed as though the Navy was calling my name. I dreamed about wearing those white bell bottoms and if I could get you to sit for a moment you can bet your last dollar I was going to tell you all about my dreams. So at the ripe old age of seventeen, I made a life time decision to join the Navy. Of course this went against the wishes of my parents. They kept telling me there was more to the Navy then a pair of bell bottom pants.

I was too young to use my own signature so this meant I had to try and convince my parents going into the Navy would be a great opportunity for me, and how seeing the world would give me a better perspective on life. They looked at me like I had bumped my head. But I was determined to get in the Navy.

So not only did I not listen to their advice, like fools my buddy and I forged our parent's signatures on the enlistment documents and on June 28, 1971 we were on our way to a place called boot camp and the rest is my story.

∽

The magical date (June 28, 1971) finally arrived. It was time for me and my buddy to face the music. So on a warm summer morning we made our way to the recruiter's office to honor our unforeseen commitment to become sailors.

The fact of the matter was neither of our parents knew what we had done. They wouldn't have ever given us their permission to join the Boy Scouts let alone the Navy.

We had both tried running these ideas pass our folks earlier that week and their responses were less than favorable.

With failure they had tried explaining to us what we were getting ourselves into. Of course we thought the people we called Mom and Dad were too old fashion and didn't understand the new hip generation.

What was it we use to sing back in the sixties, oh yeah that's it, *"Give peace a chance"*.

The old folks had a saying, you made your bed hard now you have to lay in it, never the less we were on our way.

To where, wasn't important to Buttons and myself, we just wanted to get away from our small town we called home to see this thing called the world.

As I look back over time, I realize the world and its people are the same no matter where you go.

Have you ever had an idea that wasn't thought all the way through but is seemed good at the time, well this was a classic blunder.

Not only did we not know where we were going I mean that literally, we were totally unaware of the obligation we had agreed to.

We wanted to leave our little town so bad it never dawn on us to read the fine print. Since neither one of us finished high school, between the both of us reading at best was minuscule.

To join the Navy at the age of seventeen was one thing, but dropping out of school to be all we could be, HOW DUMB WAS THAT!

The old saying, hind sight is 20/20 rings true for me because in my particular case going into the Navy turned out to be the best idea I've ever had.

But I must admit dropping out of school to do so shows how immature and naive I really was.

With all my accomplishments and formal education, I still regret that forty year old decision. I often find myself wishing I could go back to the young impressionable man to talk to him, just to get him to see how starting something new without finishing the old is a mistake.

At that time I couldn't see how finishing high school on time would be reflected as the most important event of my life.

So on that early morning of *June 28, at 5 o'clock am* Buttons and I snuck out of our houses.

We took what little belongings we had and made our way down the railroad tracks to meet our recruiter to take our first flight of life. When I say first flight of life I'm not speaking metaphorically.

Our little town didn't have an airport so we had to go to the nearest large town to catch our plane.

The details on whether we were sworn in before we got to the airport or after we arrived are still a bit hazy to me. Anyways, by 7:00 am that morning, two naive little boys were sworn in as young men into the Navy.

No turning back now, we were on our way to this place called boot camp.

We left so early in the morning, excited to start this new life that our parents didn't even have a clue we were missing.

As kids in this small town every one knew everyone so we had a lot of freedom and getting up early to play or collect junk for pocket change was a normal pattern for us.

It wasn't until a nosey neighbor told my Mother she saw me and Jerry (Buttons real name) walking towards downtown early that morning carrying what seem like knapsacks that they knew anything.

Hearing this news confirmed my Mother's suspicions that I had gone against her wishes and joined the Navy, and the hunt was on.

Don't forget, we didn't have our parent's permission to leave their homes. It took my Mother all of two weeks to locate me through the Red Cross.

I found out later she had help from my older sister Margaret who had joined the Air Force six months prior to my crazy decision to leave home.

CHAPTER 2

BOOT CAMP

One day while exercising I was called to the front building to discuss my leaving home without my parents consent or permission.

Thank GOD they found me when they did; I was in way over my head.

The stories I could tell you about boot camp alone, makes the little boy inside me still tremble with fear.

For me boot camp was no joke, someone hollering in your face while spit showered your whole person wasn't my idea of saving my country. Who ever came up with the slogan "Join the Navy to See the World" needs their ass kicked!

The Navy's basic training, should have prepared me for how this country really viewed its people. I was too young to make heads or tails of the real personality of what I thought was my country.

Many young men my age had what we call common sense, but as for me I was too young and naïve to understand. One thing I did quickly learn was that the Navy was a hiding place for misfits including myself. Some of the guys were in the Navy to escape a life of crime while others were there to start a career.

As for me, I was just trying to get away from a Mother and Father that screamed and fussed all the time, I guess the joke was on me.

As I was saying before I digressed, one day while exercising I was called to the office of the commander to discuss my leaving home without my parents consent or permission.

Needless to say these high ranking officers were pissed at me because I was illegally in their arm forces.

The thought of a seventeen year old boy forging his way into this man's Navy didn't set well with the powers to be. I was called down stairs to meet the big boys and while standing there "Pop Tall", I could hear that they had my Mother on the other line.

Shortly after my appearance they started interrogating me, they would stop periodically to ask Mom what she wanted to do, because I was only seventeen years old and still a minor my Mother's wishes would over ride Uncle Sam's contract.

If she told them to send me back home the Navy would have to release their grip on my life and comply.

Well you don't know my Mother at all, when they asked the question I was waiting for, do you want us to send him home, I had already started packing my bags in my mind.

Then I heard the craziest thing a kid could hear coming out his Mama's mouth, these three words, "**nah keep**

him"; I think I loss consciousness after that low blow to the groin.

Wait! That's not all, on my way down to my knees I could faintly hear her say something totally ridiculous and uncalled for, before she hung up the phone her last words echoed over the whole base, *"**keep him and make a man out of him"**.*

Even Joe Frasier got an eight count when Ali knocked him down. All I got was some sneers and laughter while they hauled my **(ass**-id-u-ous) behind back to the war.

My heart sunk, I just couldn't bring myself to believe this lady I called Mom could betray me like this.

A woman's intuition is good, but a Mother's instinct, is even better, so I spent the next seven years in the Navy even though I only had a three year stint.

I wasn't ready to even hear about the life of a sailor so how in heaven was I to live as a sailor only God knew this answer.

As you can tell I started out wrong and that became my way of life.

It seems every dumb thing that could happen to a person found me and parked on my street.

And before long I was nothing but trouble until I met Susan, or at least that's what I thought.

CHAPTER 3

SUSAN

My first real tour of duty was in a place called **Corpus Christi** in the state of Texas. From watching old cowboy movies I didn't think people even lived in Texas, I thought it was a place for oil rigs and a bunch of cows; was I in for a surprise.

When I arrived in Corpus it was cold, the date was October 19th and man I was instantly depressed.

I had never seen so much water, the only water I saw back home was the rock quarry.

There were these ugly planes flying all over the place making the most ungodly noises I've ever heard.

I had on my dress blues which were too tight, a pair of nylon socks not to mention those stupid patent leather shoes. These shoes weren't fit to hold a place in the shoe box they came in let alone being used to protect a set of confused feet such as mine.

Since I hadn't turned eighteen yet and had gotten all the flack about being in this man's Navy it was a perfect excuse to make the base my only stomping ground.

I couldn't go to clubs off base, but I could go to the NCO's club on base. From time to time me and some of the older guys would go to the part of town we called the cut.

Now that was a crazy ass place, all the hustlers and pimps and other low life frequent this place.

One day while standing in a store this pimp had beaten this girl and the next day her sister came in the store and blew his head off with a shotgun. So you see a lot of my time was spent on base with the other young children we called dependents (*the children of the people who were serving in the arm forces*).

Because I was afraid to go off base most of the people I knew either lived on base or visited on a regular.

I met this chick name Becky and she love to dance, so every Friday night she would come to the base to flirt with the sailors and dance with me, boy could I dance, it was through Becky I met Susan.

After I got to know Becky a little better we started doing other things on base like bowling. I remember this one particular night we had made plans to meet over to the bowling alley on base.

To my surprise Becky brought this beautiful smiling young woman and she introduced us and we bowled a few games and talked about all kinds of stuff.

I thought she was cute, but that was about all there was to the evening.

The fact that she introduced me to this pretty young lady didn't faze me, I'm not even sure I remembered her saying her name was Susan.

Susan was a dream come true, but for the life of me neither me nor my cell mates I mean bunk mates, could figure out what she saw in me.

For one thing I was younger than she was not to mention I didn't have a clue what to do with myself, let alone a woman, and a beautiful woman at that.

It just goes to show you beauty is in the eye of the beholder, what ever that means.

On August, 3rd, 1971 up to this date I had never had a real girlfriend or dated anyone except in my dreams.

Anyways, that evening I received a call from one of the boys who lived in room 226, we lived in a building called the barracks. For those of you that have never been in the arm forces the barracks is a high class jail with few exceptions.

Well when you're young anything can be distorted so I digress. This place we called the crib was a building that housed close to a hundred sailors. So to keep us organized each person was assigned a room along with three other unknown strange individuals.

The rooms were numbered from two hundred and up, me and my boys lived in room no. 222.

We called each other by last name and your room number, so as I was saying the boys from room 226 were telling me some beautiful woman was down stairs looking for me.

Because of my age these guys were always teasing me about women, so I took this as one of their jokes and didn't respond.

After about ten minutes Big Red from 226, another friend of mine, came to my room and asked me why was I keeping this lady downstairs waiting and for me to carry my ass downstairs and talk to her.

I kind of shrug him off and continue listening to my Isaac Hayes Black Moses album.

Come on people I was young, and dumb was my middle name; anyways this was all new to me.

Thirty minutes pass and tall Moses from 226 came back to my room for the second time to find out what was taking me so long.

Hind sight again is 20/20, it's clear to me now they wanted to see how I was going to handle this situation, these cats were always looking out for me because I was so young and straight off the train.

Tall Moses told me if I didn't go see what this lady wanted he was going to try and talk to her for himself, those were the rules of the barracks if you snooze, you lose.

Long story short, I went downstairs and I saw a friend of mine name Becky, she asked me if I remembered the beautiful lady she was with the night we were all bowling and I said "yes what about her", well Becky said "she wants to meet you and she thinks you're cute".

"Yeah right" I said, so I'm waiting for the punch line to this joke but it never came, Becky turns and starts walking out the door and I ask her "where are you going?" She said "to the car" and she motion for me to follow her. As I passed by a gantlet of friends, I remember one of my best friend's, Diovla saying "I don't know why she wants you, but go for it man".

The next part of this story is a blur because when I laid eyes on this creature called Susan the world stopped and I got off.

I was every man's envy that evening, a few had already tried their luck and my date had graciously turned them down.

I later found out she simply said "I'm waiting on George."

The way to describe this event is to refer to the song by the Ohio Players "**Heaven Must Be Like This**".

We spent the rest of the evening talking about any and every thing. What was a mystery to me then is very clear to me now.

It wasn't until I was much older that I figured out what Susan wanted, but that's my little secret.

After talking with her through the night and well into the morning we decided to become a couple.

So the next months were strange to me, imagine this, I had a girlfriend but wasn't sure what to do with her.

Now, I know all you heavyweight lovers in the house just got stupid, I can hear your thoughts. Most of you are saying to yourself or even out loud, "I would have blan-ketty blanked that woman". Sure you would have, that's why she was presented to me and not you.

As I was saying that next six months to a year I spent with Susan was strange, everybody I knew was asking me how we were doing and if I had gotten physical with her yet, and blah blah blah blah.

I guess the old saying is true; the same thing that can make you happy can make you sad.

At first I didn't pay their running off at the mouth much attention. I wrote it off as my boys just looking out for me, but the days turned into weeks and the weeks turned into months the inquiries got old and it didn't take long before it became bothersome.

You want to know something really funny; I didn't really know any thing about being in love. The deepest feelings I've ever had for a woman was my Mother. So as far as I was concerned Susan and I were just hanging out having fun.

With others constantly getting in my business I started looking at my situation differently.

What happen next was crazy, I fell in love with a stranger in a strange place and what was a game to me became a serious problem.

The entire time while we dated I was looking over my shoulder so to speak, I was trying to please others while desperately holding on to my new status symbol, what a mess.

Now don't forget I was still young and I had run away from home.

Out of all the places I could have run, I picked a woman's arms.

I never thought I deserved her, which was the mind of an immature undeveloped boy faced with a man's responsibility.

My so called friends didn't help matters much with their jealous remarks. Every time she would come and pick me up for a date it never failed, some small minded insignificant jerk felt it was his appointed duty to inform me on how fine they thought she was and how undeserving I was.

The mind is a powerful tool, if you're told a lie long enough you'll start to believe it. You know I started being convinced of that dumb ass shit I was hearing.

This goddess spent about a year with me while she was obviously coming out of a comma, every so often I would check the local news to see if her face would flash across the TV with those words on the bottom of the screen stating that she was missing from a mental institution and her family was hoping some one would help her find her way home. I never did see any such report so I continued dating her; however, something out of the norm did happen.

THE PHONE CALL!

I got a phone call from guess who, my Mother (sigh), mind you we weren't on good speaking terms (remember her last words "**nah keep him and make a man out of him**") so I reluctantly listened, after all she was my Mother.

She starts telling me about these dreams she was having involving me and some lady.

When she described the lady it sounded a lot like Susan so I pulled the phone tighter to my ear so as not to miss one syllable.

Ok hold up, let me explain something about my Mother, as long as I can remember she had this incredible sense of seeing things in her dreams, this might throw some of you, but for the ones that know what I am talking about let me continue the story.

As I was saying I get this phone call, did I mention it was my Mother?

So as I'm listening to the many things she shared with me about her dreams I was fully aware that her dreams were right on the money.

My heart sunk; because it became painfully obvious to me that my real first love of my life was slowly coming to an end.

Now the unbelievers will ask the question how I got all this from a single phone call, my answer to that is you don't know my Mother. Once she says she going to put the Lord on it, it's a done deal.

As a Mother she feared for my life and rightfully so, I was in way over my head and couldn't see past Susan's big blue eyes.

The next phase of this saga started with another phone call. Before the second phone call from Susan I hadn't told anyone what my Mother and I discussed on that day of wakening.

So when I got a message Susan was on the phone it took what seem like a million years for me to get to the phone because I could sense in my heart this would be the last time I would hear from my love.

THE SECOND PHONE CALL!

So I answered the phone and sure enough it was Susan, "Hello, Hi George it's me Susan".

I responded, "Hello (sigh) how are you doing this beautiful day", "not well" she said, "I have something to tell you and the thought of it makes me very sad".

It took everything I had to wait a whole second before I started begging her not to leave me and break up, how could she do this to our unborn children; come to think of it you have to have sex to make babies, that hasn't happened.

I was to in love and beside I was only eighteen years old, but that was back in 1971 not 2000, times were different then we had a different type of respect for our women.

That's another story, getting back to Susan, we were on the phone and I was begging her not to leave me, well up to now she hadn't told me why she called.

I was working off the conversation my Mother and I had a few days earlier.

For the life of me I couldn't escape the last words my Mother left ringing in my ears, "**she's no good for you, I don't want to see you get hurt**", and then came the whammy!

To say I was a mess from these two women's phone conversation would have been an understatement of the year. I listened to what Susan had to say and I started trying to figure a way pass my first love's decision to leave me, to make her see how much I loved and needed her while totally disregarding the warning from my Mother.

In the conversation with my Mother, Mom started listing all the things I was doing thousand of miles away and there was no way she could have known this stuff because I hadn't talk to her since boot camp.

This woman knew things I hadn't thought of, she even knew the color of Susan's car. Remember she had help locating me in boot camp, but there was no one here that could be telling her any thing because very few people knew where I was from, we all lied about our backgrounds.

My Mother said she saw me with this woman and I was driving this green car (Susan had a green 1971 Monte Carlo) and my Mom went on to say the car belonged to a lady who's Mother didn't like me and this lady worked in a place where she knew people that could get me in some serious trouble.

Are you confused yet, well there's more, I had never met Susan's Mother nor did I know who she worked for, but I made it my business to ask her the next time I saw her where her Mother worked.

Come to find out Susan's Mother worked for a judge in the main courthouse in town so that started me thinking about the other things Mom had mention she had saw in this dream. Can I say this, love is not only blind it's addictive and I was hooked on a drug called Susan love.

Anyways, the phone call from Susan was one of the last times I saw or heard from her, she moved five hundred miles from me and was never heard of again.

CHAPTER 4

GIVONNI

Have you ever heard the old saying true love is just an arm length away, well neither had I until I saw my second love and my first wife to be months after recovering from the sinking ship called Susan love.

Remember I'm a sailor; I use a lot of Navy metaphors.

Here's one of the most sexist of all, as one ship pulls out to sea another pulls in to take its place.

My second love didn't come easy, to be honest I was still hurt from my previous relationship and to be quite frank I was what we call damaged goods.

During my whole time with Susan I had other friends that were in the Navy who just happen to be Waves (Women in the Navy). This one particular lady was friends of Doivla and we spent a lot of time together.

The women's barrack was next to the men's, needless to say there were always a sailor or two visiting and I was no exception.

Pat was a pretty cool chick; she was easy to talk to and had a beautiful heart. Doivla fell in love with her, he once told me because she cried a lot. Have you every seen one of those people that wanted to save the world, well that was Doivla.

Because she was so easy going people took advantage of her and this gave Doivla all the reason he needed to wear his red cape.

Anyways she had this little friend the complete opposite of herself name Givonni. She stood four feet eleven, weighed about a hundred pounds soaking wet, had the brain power of Albert Einstein, had a quick tongue, sharp as a tack and was a freaking feminist. She once told me women should be in charge of the world because men suck! Outside of these small infractions she was cool.

From time to time I would see her around base and when the opportunity presented itself I would speak in passing but never tried to hold any type of conversation with her, she had a reputation for ripping men heads off and handing it back to you on a sliver platter.

As I got to know her better I found out why she felt that way. I tried for close to twenty five years to help heal her scars and never even came close; we'll get into that later on in the story.

As I was saying I didn't like her too much, when I first started observing her from a distance. She was quick to tell you how she felt about you and I didn't need that in my life.

I heard her tell this big dude with a smile his cologne stunk, and that when he was around her it would be nice if he considered not wearing the stuff.

I love talking to Pat and would even peek at her back-side when she wasn't looking. For some reason we would always end up talking about the small evil one.

This is an over exaggeration I'm writing a book so I'm trying to keep it funny and exciting.

As you can imagine Givonni was a fire ball. Let me wind this story back a few sentences, keep in mind that I had quit high school to join the Navy plus I was from this small country town in the Midwest, did I tell you I couldn't read?

It's true the person writing this book at the age of nineteen could not read. I just needed to clarify that fact before I tell how Givonni became my hero.

∽

Getting back to the story, I saw Givonni going into the NCO's club one night and it was at that instance I wanted to ask her to marry me, why I don't know, I think I was being funny, that joke lasted for years to come.

If this next part of the story seems convoluted that is because it was, this whirlwind of a life I was caught up in was moving too fast for the kid, but I held on and when October the 19, 1973 came around Givonni and I were wedded.

On the ride down to the courthouse we keep checking to see if we were doing the right thing. Givonni and I had talked about this date for six months or so, finally we convinced ourselves it was the right thing to do.

We arrived at our destination, walked inside and then we found out we needed a witness. So I went outside the justice of the peace office and found this drunken guy and ask him if he wanted to witness a wedding. He said "yeah" and there we stood in front of God and country, we said our "I do's" and I remember the feeling of being lost sweeping over both of us, what the hell did we just do.

After the courthouse experience both of us went back to our respective rooms in the barracks even though we had a little apartment right off base for some reason we needed to be alone.

The story on how we started living together seems a bit long, but all of this happen months after I first saw and started talking to Givonni. I knew very little about her. I know this sounds crazy, even while I'm writing this story I don't believe it myself.

One of the reasons we got married so fast was other people were doing it, another reason was the Navy paid you more money if you were married.

I was sleep in my room when one of my friends came in and ask if it was true that I had gotten married today, and I answer him saying "yes", he told me to get my ass out the barracks and go get my wife and go home.

He went on to let me know that those days when I could stay around the crib was some what over. The first few weeks were crazy, but we managed to make it.

June 28, 1974, the magical date, this was the date for my release. The closer I got to this date the more I wanted to make the Navy my home.

Because of my previous years and the problems I caused, the Navy didn't want me.

In fact, I can remember Mr. Bayshore, the squadron First Officer telling me he wish he could find a way to get the Navy to put me in jail to get back some of the time I had wasted. But they had decided against it. The fact of the matter was the base's captain and I had gotten close, we would sit and talk for hours about life.

Being I was so young, the Captain was always encouraging me to do my best. The first time the words leadership and my name were put in the same sentence was from the mouth of this man I called captain.

It's one thing to hear words like leadership, honor, duty, and country but I know now it takes a special person to receive and understand it.

He would always say, "Harris, you got good potential don't waste it by getting in trouble with those other guys."

In fact it was this man who thought enough of my ability to lead others to use my talent when there was a misunderstanding between the establishment and the soul brothers.

He would call me to go and speak with my friends to see if there was anything the Navy could do to make their stay on base a little more comfortable. The first time I was told to come to the captain's office I was scared to death, but I digress.

∽

Getting back to June 28, 1974 the magical date of my release, I remember waking up early that morning and feeling sad and excited, about becoming a civilian.

Before I tell the rest of the story let me go back a couple of years and tell you why the Navy didn't want me to sign my name on the dotted line for another three years.

You know about the illegal way I got in the Navy in the first place. Remember I signed my Mother and Father's name on the dotted line and as far as I was concerned that was how you did things, if you wanted something lie and cheat to get it.

So my time spent in the Navy until I got married was very spotted to say the least, to make a long story short I became one big pain in the ass.

Besides entering the Navy without my parent's consent, I was a naive loud mouth brat that thought he knew it all. I was so wet behind the ears you know those paper towels called the quicker picker upper; I could have used a case of them and still had enough wetness to supply Niagara Falls. My attitude was crazy. It took me another thirty years to change how I did things, but that's another story.

CHAPTER 5

CIVILIAN LIFE A MILITARY WIFE

Givonni on the other hand had more time to serve, so some decisions had to be made, if she was too continue her Navy career what was I to do, hum?

However, we hadn't given much thought to this question but, this didn't stop the fact we were going to have to make some kind of decision, so we decided she should stay in while I become her dependent.

The next leg of my journey took Givonni and me to a place so crazy I don't have words to describe how we felt upon arrival to this place called Italy. Here's the deal, the Navy requires all sailors do sea duty, usually that means going aboard a ship for two years or so.

At the time we were in the Navy women weren't allowed on ships so you had to pick a place that could be considered sea duty so we picked Italy.

Now what we knew about Italy was spaghetti and meat balls. After making the decision to go, Givonni and I spent many nights trying to figure out how we were going to live in a place where the people didn't speak English.

The more we thought about it the more crazy this idea was. Too late now the orders were cut, by this time next month we were going to be in our new home away from home, Italy.

Everything about this place was strange to us, neither of us knew how far Italy was from the United States of America, but we wanted to go to Europe. Let me put this crazy idea in some kind of perspective. We had just got married in October of 1973 and here now in August in 1974 not even a full year later two people that were practically strangers to each other were about to travel half way across the world to do what?

Looking back we were some strong people to even think we could pull this off. The time to leave came on August 12, 1974, we boarded a plane to cross the Atlantic Ocean, a twelve or fourteen hour trip to our new world called Italy.

We arrived in Rome early afternoon and a thing called culture shock met us at the terminal. To start with there were no terminals, and as far as the airport was concerned the plane couldn't pull up to the building, so we were let off in the middle of the runway and we had to walk to the building.

It seems some fool took it upon himself to bomb the airport. We got inside and there were armed soldiers everywhere, walking around with machine guns ready to shoot.

The first few days in this new foreign place was very traumatic for us. You see we kind of looked at going to

Italy as a honeymoon, we had pictured this whole romantic scene, you know clinking glasses full of rich red wine, the smell of delicious bread and pasta everywhere.

Well that bubble was burst at the airport, damn! Welcome to the real Italy. Both our limited views of the world were too naive to know any truths; we thought we had left the violence back in America. The scene at the airport was just a wake up call, but the real deal was yet to come.

Our sponsor was this guy name Kenny Huff, he finally arrived and not a minute too soon. Givonni and I were freaking out, it seemed to us we had made a wrong choice, we thought these people we call Italians were crazy.

The fact that they all talked really loud and at the same time wasn't a problem, I was use to loud folks because my family, had this same trait. This scene reminded me of our family reunions loud talking and to outsiders it seemed like a fight was about to break out. Kenny never took a second look with a smirk and a smile he simply helped us load our belongings into his car and we were off to Naples.

When we got to Naples it was dirty and very busy, I had never been in a city before and Naples had a reported number of five million people. It seems all five million were out on the street going about their every day life.

There were people selling all kinds of merchandise in the street, I mean literally in the street. Imagine if you will a side street filled with merchants selling everything, food, clothes, shoes, fake jewelry and in some cases your basic dreams of tomorrow.

Well I'm exaggerating about the dream thing, but I'm not kidding it felt like we had stepped into an episode from "**The Twilight Zone**".

Here you had these tiny streets with barely enough room for two people to pass without rubbing elbows and we were being told these were regular streets for cars.

Since I mention the elbow rubbing thing, let me explain a subtle difference in our culture here in America compared to the rest of the world.

Our society here in America promotes what is called a *"Bubble Society"*. All this really means is, we in this country are afraid to get up close and personal with each other, we all feel the need to have personal space which explains why we're so damn selfish.

In other parts of the world you have what is called a *"Bumping Society"*. What this means is you're always touching and rubbing up against one another. Getting use to these small cultural differences took some time, but before we knew it we were touching with the best of them.

Coming from a poor midsize family I had plenty of practice rubbing and touching because private space hadn't been invented yet. We never had separate beds, at times there would be three people to a bed, so privacy was something you saw on the *"Leave it to Beaver Show"*. I never slept in my own bed until I got in the Navy.

Getting back to what I was saying about the different types of society, we in America love our big cars and big houses, but we isolate ourselves from each other.

Well the Italians have a different look on the car thing, they try and fit as many cars on the road as possible, so of course they bump and touch quite frequently.

Driving in a foreign country requires getting what is called an international license. To qualify for this license, all Americans were required to take a course which was nothing short of a class to help all new comers to adjust to the idea of being one of thousands of motorists on the street at the same time.

It's during these classes you learn that having an accident is inevitable, so its not if you have an accident, it's when you have one. I can't tell you how many accidents I had during my stay in Italy; in some cases I was involved in more then two the same day.

I know I'm jumping all over the place taking you from the scene at the airport to how the Italians drove their cars even to making a comparison about the differences in our cultures.

However, I want to try and get you to see through Givonni and my eyes just how bizarre this Alice and Wonderland trip was to us.

Remember we hadn't long gotten married and we didn't know each other at all. We were both very young and fresh off the farm.

So to try and capture our first night in this rabbit hole is a little hazy to me.

The ride from Rome to Naples was nice; looking at the country side it was easy to see this place had a rich history full of culture. Some of the world's greatest artist came from this part of the world Michael Angelo, Leonardo Givenchy, Sofia Loren, and the list goes on for miles.

Givonni and I noticed the further we traveled south of Rome the dirtier this country got and the less courteous the drivers became.

By the time we arrived in Naples we figure out this must be where they shipped all the bad drivers. Man this stuff was crazy, traffic lights and stop signs didn't have much meaning here.

And as far as pedestrians were concerned you cross at your own risk. Crossing the street was like something out of the keystone cop's movie, where a person tries to cross the road and it seems drivers are trying to get as close as they can to them without making contact.

We were peeking from behind closed eyes while softly screaming out of fear waiting for the sound a car makes when it hits a human body, of course Kenny was use to this kind of human dodge ball and he navigated through the maze of cars and people without one incident.

The whole time we spent in Italy I only heard of one incident involving a pedestrian and a car. Another thing you rarely saw or heard of was fatal car crashes.

Kenny took us to a hotel and this place was a mess, but he informed us we were only spending the night here and tomorrow we were to check into a much better place across the street from NAS, the military base. The Navy wanted you to be close to other Americans just arriving in country to lessen the affects of such a devastating culture shock.

We didn't know it yet but those words were some of the best things we heard all day. Upon our arrival to the first hotel, Givonni and I noticed swat stickers were spray painted all over the front of the hotel. Now I may not have been able to speak Italian, but I knew enough to know these symbols meant trouble.

And to top it off we were totally unaware of the fact that this place was right in front of a city zoo with lions, tigers and bears. I'm not kidding, after our return to the hotel from spending our first night on the town with our new friends the Huff's, we were awaken around three o'clock in the am by the sound of lions roaring and elephants blowing their horns.

Don't forget we had just flew fourteen hours across the Atlantic ocean so we were jet lag and to add to our shock most of my clothes were still on a boat making their way to Italy, don't ask me how that happened it just did. All I remember is I had to wear some of Givonni's shirts for the next two days.

So the words just for the night were the best thing we had heard that whole day. So it's worth me repeating the fact that Kenny informing us we would be moving into the hotel we would stay in until we found an apartment was a life saver.

So he helped us with our bags and said he would come back later to pick us up to take us to his house to meet his family. We freshened up and got something to eat. While sitting in the lobby of the hotel, we met other new arrivals and shared stories, before long Mr. Huff returned just as he promised.

The Huff's were a great family, Mrs. Huff was an Italian national she was from Sicily, Kenny on the other hand had lived in Italy for a number of years and spoke the language fluently, and we couldn't have been in better hands.

We talked about the Italian culture and drank different types of wine and ate a real Italian dish for the first time, Danielle could really cook. We made it through our first night. When the alarm went off our bodies were telling us it was two o'clock in the am so we struggled to get out of bed, what motivated us was the thought of being thousand of miles from home in a place most people only dreamed of.

It's true, a good night's sleep or good day's sleep depending on how you look at it can make a difference. Kenny came to the hotel and picked us up and I told him about the strange noises we heard during the wee hours of the night. He looks at me with a cigarette hanging from his mouth and said "oh yeah the hotel sets practically in the city zoo".

Well the first day turned into another which turned into weeks then months. Mean time and between times we ourselves became sponsors of other couples coming to Italy.

Needless to say we fell in love with the whole country and its people. When the time came to leave we felt we were leaving our childhood world behind.

Givonni and I had gotten to know some of the greatest people in the world right in our own backyard. Like Mr. Williams who lived up stairs, he had an interesting life.

It took me awhile to put two and two together. He had been deported from America while living in New York, I'll just stop there, you can figure out the rest. He was a family man for those of you that are real slow.

Mr. Williams was one of many who played a significant part in two young American lives. The time came for me and Givonni to leave our first love and I must admit we hated to go, but had a taste for McDonalds' Big Mac and fries. The golden arches were always calling us like an old friend in the far off distance, so we said our good byes and made our way to Norfolk Virginia.

CHAPTER 6

WELCOME "BACK" TO AMERICA

The first night we spent in America was in Philadelphia, man talking about culture shock again. Now this place was filthy. The streets were crowded, the people talked to fast and loud, and every policeman had these big ass guns strapped to their side like it was the Wild Wild West.

An amazing thing happen, we found it more difficult to get back in the swing of things when we returned to good old U.S. of A. We never dream home would end up being some place where we didn't feel we belonged.

Many of the friends we had while in Italy had been shipped out and ended up in Norfolk, so when we return it was like we had sponsors again. Since they all had made this transition months before us they thought it was funny we didn't want to speak English when going to a simple place like McDonalds.

I can remember the first time we went to McDonalds the people behind the counter would say "hi welcome to McDonalds, may I take your order please" and we would turn to our friends and tell them in Italian what we wanted, they in turn would translate in English what we wanted.

We couldn't speak Italian as well as we spoke English, it's just we had gotten use to hearing Italian when we went out to eat and a great amount of time was spent learning how to speak the language to the point it was just hard to turn this translating thing off.

It hit me the hardest because while we were in Italy I was a civilian so I spent a lot of time off base dealing with all sorts of different type of characters, you name it I was doing it.

I remember one time I was dropping off some goods I had for a friend of mine, and being young I didn't know any better so I made the mistake of asking the question where all this stuff was going and who picked up this merchandise after we left it in this underground warehouse.

Mr. V. looks at me kind of strange as he proceeded to tell me not to ask questions I really didn't want to know the answers to. I was young, but somewhat of a quick learner so I change the topic to the weather and never asked again.

He went on to say as long as we held up our end of the bargain everything would be fine. After these little escapades, we would go to his house, eat pasta and drink wine until it was time for me to return to the base; that's where I made all my connections.

∽

Back at Norfolk, Givonni and I were trying our damnedest to find any reason to go back overseas. Life in

America wasn't working for us. Around this time the Navy was starting to change their policy about women aboard ships.

Up to now the Navy didn't demand Waves to go aboard ships to fulfill their sea duty obligation, as soon as this went into effect we started looking for ways to end our Navy career and get back to the real life as an American civilian.

While Givonni finished out her term with the Navy I went back to school. For the longest time I wanted to work with electrical equipment like computers.

I was sitting one day watching TV when this commercial caught my attention. This little old ugly man saying, do you want to change your life and make a lot of money while living your wildest dream? I thought to myself here comes the old *okee-dokee,* by now I had learned anything that sounds too good to be true usually is.

The funny thing is, I was looking for a career and I had the G.I Bill, so I got on my bike and peddled my way into the future.

A career in computer technology, the only thing I knew about computers was they were smart. So I signed up for the classes at ECPI, a tech school and to my surprise most of the guys and girls enrolled were ex-military, so I felt right at home.

From the beginning things weren't right, all these soul brothers in the same class meant things were going to be run just a little different and different it was.

For starters we all had this attitude that since we were paying for this education via military services (the G.I. bill) no one was going to dictate to us how much we could learn or what to learn, so we took control of the classes in a subtle but strong way. This was the late 70's and the civil rights issues were still very much alive.

We soul brothers recognized education was power, and most of them joined the services to get money for college. Once we realized this school needed us to survive, and our Uncle Sam's money had a loud voice we made damn sure we got what we needed to be successful.

I believe that was one of the reasons a company named Westinghouse had come all the way from Maryland to hire us. We were the only black electronic tech school, and we were the best. Getting back to how the classes were structured. Classes started for the most part when all of us arrived. It gave each of us time to travel from different parts of the city so we held classes up until the whole crew was there; starting at the appropriate time was unheard of.

Like I said earlier, since we were using our GI bill to get this education we made damn sure we got every thing we had coming and in some instances maybe just a little more. It was a six month course, but being ex-military we were use to a strenuous regiment, so we did it in four and a half. Since the school was near two military bases, our class was culturally diverse.

This company Westinghouse got wind of it and decided they needed just such a thing to seal the deal they had for a military contract. With affirmative action and all if you as a company wanted a government contract you had to employ so many minorities.

Now how they got wind of ECPI is beyond me, but I can say this, we were told they would be coming and to be prepared to take the test to get hired and so we did for a week.

We sharpen our skills and sure enough they came with high expectations, but our class was the best.

Then something strange happen while we were waiting for the test to begin, some office politics was being conducted. They had to give us the test to make it legit, but I could almost swear the answers were already filled in their proper slots.

I'm not saying, but I'm saying something strange was going on. Anyways we were told we all passed the test and we were expected to report to the **BWI** site *(Baltimore Washington international Airport)* the following Monday morning for orientation and that was that.

∽

Let me digress for just a minute, this whole writing was inspired by the passing of my lovable wife Denise and I promise I'll get to that however, I just want to point out how funny life can be by showing how a person can say something to you and those words become life.

Hence the old saying "Be careful what you ask for you just might get it". For example, I've often thought about what was said to me by a mechanic on many occasions.

One day I was in Virginia Beach getting my car fixed and some months later I was in a place called "Charm

City", better known as **B-more.** I'm not sure if this next thought had any thing to do with my sudden change in atmosphere. Some would say it's just a coincidence, but this city had been mention to me to many times just to be a passing thought.

As I was saying I was getting my car fixed while living in Virginia Beach and the mechanic started talking to me about women. He told me if you ever wanted to see some beautiful black chicks go to B-more.

The first time I heard this city's vernacular was in boot camp. There was this cat named James, he wore his Navy hat cock to the side and when he walk it seem like he had a limp, he called this pimping.

Any who he would start talking about this place called B-more and he wouldn't shut up. He talk as if this place was the best place in the world, I didn't get it. I asked him one time why the hell anyone would want to live in a place where you couldn't park your car without some other low life fool stealing it and he called this fun.

I remember that was one of the things I hated about Italy, you couldn't leave your car parked outside in fear some A-hole would steal it, the same old stuff different place.

If James was the best they had to offer well, let's just say they could do better. I couldn't help but think if all Baltimoreans acted like this dude I wanted to stay as far from there as possible.

Back to the garage talk, getting involved with any woman at this time of my life was the last thing on my mind, another woman; he didn't know I already had a wife.

This guy kept singing these high praises about how beautiful Baltimore's women were to the point I found my thoughts straying. The power of suggestion can be a dangerous thing. The fact that I'm writing about it some forty years later lets you know the impression it made on me, hum, a woman of color. Not even eight months later after the conversation with the mechanic I found myself in of all places Baltimore (B-more). City life wasn't my idea of good living, in fact living in Naples Italy with a population of 5 million people, was insane. I believe in living in harmony but inner city life, now that's straight crazy.

The hustle and bustle, the constant clamoring of people, and lack of concern, what a mess; I had never been in a city where the population was 80% black. Talking about your culture shock, there was plenty to go around. After arriving in Baltimore I was quickly reminded of the first time Givonni and I went to Amsterdam.

Here we were thousands of miles from America, but the people all dressed and acted like they were in a city like New York. I was shocked then too, but Amsterdam wasn't as dirty as this place or Naples. It has always puzzled me, why do people trash where they live? I'll leave that thought to the geniuses of the world.

∽

Givonni was still in the Navy so I had to leave her behind. She and I were already having marital problems. It's easy to blame it on the fact we got married way to young, but the truth was we never learn how to treat each other as husband or wife.

Looking back over the entire mess I have to point the finger at myself. Some of you might ask the question how's that possible, when it takes two to tangle. You know that's a fair enough assessment and here's why I take the blame.

In every relationship someone has to take the lead and I just happen to believe the man should be that person, but there are exceptions.

I would like to share a short story with you in reference to how leadership should always be on duty.

Being that I was in the Navy I was always around or on aircraft carriers, they're the big ones.

The weather man had called for severe weather so we batten down the hatches and made sure everything was secured.

In the wee hours of the night the storm slithered into the harbor like a thief, with mild thunder roaring off into the distance, with an occasional flash of lighting marking its spot.

As the evening changed into to early morning the once quiet storm turns into forceful winds on full blast rocking our city on water. Some how with all the movement of the ocean our ship broke free of its anchor and drifted into a neighboring ship causing major damage. The whole time this was happening the captain was in his quarters asleep. The men on duty that night were well equipped to handle the matter and they did.

At the orders of the XO, second in command they moved the ship back to its original place and started repairs. To our surprise the next day the Capitan was relieved of duty, to the crew this was very unfair because he was a good officer. But to the Navy he had lost control of his ship and was no longer fit to command a vessel.

When we ask for a reason for this decision we were told that a captain should always know what's going on aboard his ship even if he's asleep, now that's some heavy stuff.

So if I'm the man in the relationship and it runs a ground, I feel it's my responsibility and I'm to blame. As a captain of destiny I should know at all times the direction we're going. Even if it was told to me by my wife, I should know, and then take control of the marriage and guide it in the proper direction to keep it safe and I did not do that.

So by 1982 my marriage was running in the wrong direction, I had plotted a bad course years ago and the fruit of my indecision was coming back to haunt me.

By 1984 I had ran us aground, it was over, so I abandoned ship and did the unthinkable I left my mate with a broken ship unworthy for sea duty. I don't have the time to fill in all the blanks and to be honest with you it hurts to write the truth and I would much rather skim over it and get to the part I call better times. But you know what, I still hadn't learn my lesson because even though I had left my marriage in my mind I was still obligated to Givonni because we were still married.

I continued to pay my bills and take care of the financial stuff, but I totally neglected a beautiful woman's heart. I started wandering, which was nothing new for me. The nitty gritty and dirt throwing part of our marriage shall remain a mystery, there's way too many tears involved to share that story's entirety however, I will share this. I was a problem if you recall early in the story. I said it took me some thirty years to learn how to conduct myself as a responsible adult. Let's just leave it at that.

I was working at Westinghouse as you remember and Givonni had followed my lead and attended the same school ECPI as well. Money wasn't an issue for us, we made plenty of that, but as time went on we drifted further and further apart.

CHAPTER 7

DENISE

In October 1984 a new person started working in my department, what an angel. When I tell you this next part I'm not exaggerating at all. I was sitting at my station when I heard one of my colleagues saying something, I turn to see what she was say and standing next to her was this beautiful young lady.

She looked to be around twenty years old and had this glow that surrounded her body and she was smiling, it was love at first sight. If I had I dollar for every time I heard that I would still be broke, but it's true about love at first sight, at least it was for me.

She introduced herself and I knew this was going to be a special time in my life. To begin with she was a beautiful chocolate brown with a pair of almond shaped brown eyes. When she smiled it was as if heaven opened up its doors and poured out pure love. I made it known to her right then and there that she was the most beautiful black woman I had ever seen.

You know what they say, whoever they are; beauty is in the eyes of the beholder. Well on April 14, 1962 God decided to created a child name Denise, on April 14,

1952 God decided to create a child name Givonni. They were born exactly ten years apart and from two different eras, yet these two women had many things in common, but to me the most important thing was me.

༄

Givonni and I met during the Vietnam War crises when slogans like "Give Peace a Chance" really meant something. The fact that she was a Midwestern white girl and I was a Midwestern black boy had a lot to do with our decision to get married in the first place.

We had this plan; she would use her complexion to move in and out of white society, while I use my blackness to keep our partnership real with that street edge. Of course when I look back over it now I realize we were both crazy as hell.

Here's another piece of our plan, we had decided to only stay married for ten years after which we would part company and go our separate ways. So by the time I met Denise, Givonni and I had damaged our marriage so badly, it was beyond repair. I guess you really should be careful what you speak.

In our case when the ten years rolled around we were done as husband and wife. Givonni and I got married October 19, 1973 and by October of 1984, we had stopped living together. We were still in the same house, but we weren't together.

Unlike the captain I mention early in the story, life had seen fit to allow me to be re-commissioned and I got another ship (relationship).

I know I make it sound so easy and fun, but let me tell you this was no easy task. To begin with Denise didn't trust me because I was married, even though I told her I would get a divorce and marry her, yeah right.

All I really wanted was her tight young body. Remember back when I said it was love at first sight that was true. But because of my maleness I shrugged that off and turned my focus else where. She was young and impressionable and naïve, at least that's what I thought.

Sure enough as time went by we became a couple. Her family didn't quite know what to make of all this, they were fully aware of my marital status because of one of her nosey ass aunts that also worked at the Circle Bar W (Westinghouse).

∞

Come to think of it, I had a similar problem with Givonni's family. Those backward thinking people hated black people so much her Mom threaten to kick her out the family if she married me and just to spite her she married me anyways.

And as far as I was concern I would like to tell you they came around during those twenty or so years Givonni and I was married, but no such luck, they never accepted me.

Givonni and I were married from 1973 until 1995 and her family other than her brother once, never even met me. I couldn't get my head wrapped around how one human being could hate another human they had never met.

Being married to a white woman gave me a unique advantage. If I wanted to really know how certain groups of whites were thinking I would send Givonni and they would reveal themselves to her as the undercover racist they really were. This worked both ways, if I wanted to know how certain brothers and sisters were thinking I simply showed up without my white wife.

Because we were able to infiltrate either camp it taught us to only trust ourselves. Givonni and I talked about it a lot, if we got a divorce we agreed neither one of us would marry outside of our race again.

Here it is 2010 and as far as I know we have both stuck to the promises we made twenty some years ago.

I must digress for a moment; from living the first part of my adult life being involved in interracial relationships, I've learned people are stupid. I know these words are kind of harsh but it's true. Right now it's on my heart to say this, at some risk of course, but if you out there would be honest you would share with the audience how you feel about this matter.

I have two thirteen year old boys and I've already told them to stay with what they know when it comes to getting married. I would never suggest to anyone who to marry, but I'll tell you this, interracial relationships are tuff.

∽

Now where was I, oh yeah Denise, when we met she had a little daughter we called baby girl, she was four years old. I didn't have nor wanted any offspring; however, the part of me that was doing the thinking convinced me to hook up with this young Mother.

Because she had her daughter at the young age of eighteen, she was having struggles in her life. When I got to know them a little better I found out her Mom had had her at the age of fifteen.

Hold on I'm getting a bit ahead of myself, let me go back to the first night I went over to Denise's house to take her out on a date. Remember before I said money was no problem, well I had bought myself a brand new 320i BMW. I was the only brother I knew that had one so I was tripping. Anyways I showed up at 7:00 pm dress like Lionel from the Jefferson's, instead of moving on up I felt like I was moving on down because this was the ghetto.

Armed with a single red rose to try and win this woman's heart, I knocked on the door. To this day I still have that rose, pressed inside a book Denise kept as a scrap book. I didn't know it at the time, but Denise was very romantic and she was aware of her inner beauty and she was special.

We spent the night together and that was when I realize she was special because of the manner in which she took to ensure this first encounter was one of a life time and it was, to describe it in one word, extraordinary. I had never seen in real life and I definitely didn't take the time to look outside myself to think of how someone may have felt about me.

To say she blew my mind was an understatement. When I dropped her off the next day and went back to my house, the only thought that occupied my mind was when I could see this beautiful creature again.

Denise was the first woman I had been with that I didn't want to get up and leave immediately after the sex. This took me back because I had never felt these feelings before. Even when I was head over hills in love with Susan it wasn't like this. I know I was older when I met Denise, but I'm telling you she was the person I dreamed of when I was a kid. I know this may sound like a cliché, but she was the girl of my dreams.

Our first encounter was on a Friday night. This gave me all day Saturday to think of her gracefulness; her gentle soft voice; the smile in her eyes and the way she wrapped her body around me, I was sprung.

I immediately made plans to see her again and the desire to be together was surprisingly strong between us, we seem to be a match made in heaven.

She must have thought the same thing because she would always say yes. It wasn't until years later I found out she wasn't sure about those early days. When I ask why she continued to see me she said I made her laugh.

So the words can I see you tonight, became our mantra, so every chance we got we were together. I almost wish this part of the story was fiction, but it's real. At this particular time in our newly developing romance Denise and I already came into this relationship with more baggage then the lost and found at the airport.

Like her Mother for instance, lord this woman could make Jesus scream, her ability to get on your last nerve via nagging, was a work of art. When she got wind of Denise's idea to move out and the fact I had something to do with her decision caused all hell to break loose.

At one point she told Denise she could move out, but Noreen had to stay with her. This next move wasn't the brightest thing I've ever done, I went to Ellen to inform her that not only was Noreen part of a Mother daughter package, but I intended on moving in with the both of them. She cuss me smooth out, but that was cool I had said my peace.

My future Mother-in-law was only ten years older than me, she was like an older sister to me and she hated that she couldn't boss me around. In retrospect I know I was wrong. I didn't give her the respect I should have; after all she was the Mother and Grandmother.

When I got my senses back I apologized for my actions, but I kept the woman and child. The actual plan was for me to come over spend weekends with Denise and baby girl and then go back to my other house in the county. I must have been out of my mind.

Even though I had been married for ten years I must admit I knew nothing about how women processed things in their heads, it's a wonder those two women didn't get together and kick my black ass.

Living with any one woman is more than a challenge for a man and me trying to live with two women "*Damn that sounds like a monster movie! Oh I'm sorry this doesn't have any thing to do with the story I just like how it sounds*".

I can hear the women in the audience saying that wouldn't work and you're right, it didn't. I wanted to have her to myself and I was willing to help her with whatever bills she would incur, so once she moved in, so did I.

This pissed Ellen (my future Mother-in-law) off even more, not only was she about to loose her daughter to an older man; we were taking the one person she felt she had influence over, the four year old grand-daughter. I wouldn't be myself If I didn't keep this real honest even though it will expose me as well.

I did play a major part in this whole mess; to begin with I didn't like Ellen or her family at all, I just wanted Denise. This woman (Denise's Mother) was so loud and could be very obnoxious and so stupid at times it was almost unbearable.

∽

Before I drop one more syllable on this paper, let me point out the ending to this part of the story here and now. It took some years, but Denise's Mom and I eventually became great friends and we learned to love and respected each other.

Now back to the beginning, I was able to convince Denise to move away from her Mother to get her away from all that drama, not to mention we needed a place where we could spend time together. It wasn't long before I found myself at a cross road, Denise and I hearts started to become as one, but our past lives were still calling.

For instance, I was still legally married to Givonni, she and I still had financial obligations. So if we were to give this new relationship a chance all of us had to break some of our ties we had with a past life and move on, easier said than done. I was willing to do something, however, getting a divorce from Givonni seemed a bit drastic, and throwing all my chances at this newly formed arrangement scared the be jeezes out of me.

But I had to dump or get off the pot. I took the cowardly way out. I would wait for Givonni to go to work so I could sneak in our house, take the necessary amount of clothing I needed and simply disappear over to the apartment until I could explain to Givonni what I was doing.

This chain of events took about two weeks before I was man enough to face Givonni and tell her the full truth. I know how stupid this all must sound, but I never said I was the sharpest knife in the draw. So I went to Givonni and basically made a deal. I would continue making mortgage payments and she could stay in the house as long as she liked.

This arrangement lasted about three years; I couldn't continue to take care of two places. As far as these two were concerned I was doing a half ass job at both places because no man can serve two masters.

During those three years Denise, Givonni and I sat down on many occasions and talked about the situation I had place us all in.

I should have noticed how chummy they had gotten, believe me when I tell you this, I was totally unaware these two heifers were plotting against me.

Wait a minute! Who just said but of course? Lady or madam, take your hands off your hips and sit down so we can continue to read, there's one in every crowd!

Any who as I was saying before, I was so rudely interrupted; I was unaware what was going through these two women's minds.

Now I got a secret that I haven't revealed yet and that is I have a new partner and she has been reading this book as I'm writing it. One of the parts she plays in my life is to remind me of my past life's experiences. How this all came about is another story, but she pointed out one particular lady friend I dated before Denise. So here we go.

CHAPTER 8

GINA

I met her the winter of 1981. Every Christmas holiday, Westinghouse would shut down to save the company some money. This particular shutdown was no different, except months prior to closing I met and started talking to this beautiful sister name Gina.

I mostly joked around with her to try and make her laugh. When she laughed the walls of the building shook. Her crazy ass laugh could be heard from one end of the place to the other and there were two wings in this building.

Sometime it was embarrassing because her laughing drew to much attention.

Like anything the more time you spend talking the more comfortable you get and before long we found ourselves sharing sob stories; me complaining about a failed marriage that I helped destroy and her about this boy who had gotten her pregnant.

As I was saying, this was all kind of developing a few months before Christmas shutdown. One day some months earlier I was standing in the hallway with one of my elderly friends and a woman walked by. They casually spoke and she continued on her way up and around the corner. When she was out of sight he softly mention that he and she had dated for a whole year and how good the experience had been.

That idea turned me on, I thought to myself that would be so cool to have a one year fling. WRONG!!! Here again thinking with the wrong head. Through my conversation with Gina I found out her old man wasn't taking care of business and was slacking or should I say lacking in his housework.

Well she had an itch and I wanted to scratch it. Ladies let this be some what of a lesson to you, before a man can get in your panties he gets in your head. Hell, I'm just preaching to the choir ain't that right ladies.

With all this stirring in my head I had decided on our last day before shut down to ask her could we talk. With much anticipation our last day had finally arrived, good she was wearing those maroon color pants made out of that valor material that hugged her assets oh so attentively.

It was now or never, I went up to Gina and ask her what I could do to get her to be with me, and she turned and started laughing. I wanted to walk away, but I was too embarrassed so I stood there totally confused and hurt.

All the signs were there, I knew she liked me, how could I have missed my cue. I waited for her to stop cackling so I could walk away with some form of dignity. She turns towards me, all the while wiping tears from her eyes, she gave me the strangest look like she was confused and said and I repeat she said, "Nothing".

Being the gentleman I am, I just turned and walked away. All during the winter break which lasted for two weeks, this thing with lady G bothered me. I really wanted her in a bad kind of way, I'm just being honest. So our break was over and we started back to work and I avoided her every chance I could, those last words "nothing", tormented me.

Not long after startup she came to me and said "why didn't you call me over the Christmas shut down?" Man this woman was crazy, when I asked her to spend some time with me she very coldly told me no. Now she going to ask this dumb ass question, woman please. Y'all know I wanted to say something different.

But here again I wanted people to see me as a gentleman so I simply said "I asked you what I could do to get you to like me and you said nothing". Before I could finish this fool started laughing again, this time I think I cussed and started to walk off when she grab my arm. She said "fool, I said nothing because you've already done everything necessary to have me".

Hell I was done, you mean I could have been somewhere cozy with you, instead I was home wishing on a star. Life has a funny way of trying to fix itself. What I mean by that is Gina and I didn't get together until sometime later. You see we both had our own obligations, so she went her way and I went mine.

We still talked from time to time, but she was a little bit too wild for me so I was glade circumstances had provided me a way out. I went back to acting like I was happy going home sitting in the driveway not wanting to go inside. It was too much of a reminder of how screwed-up my life really had become. And the fact I was still in a marriage I wanted to get out of didn't help matters.

So I did the next best thing, I joined a group that called themselves "Aimway" the American dream. Somewhere in that twisted mind of mine I pretended this could help save what little fraction of a relationship Givonni and I had left.

༄

Getting back to Gina, we were becoming good friends. One night she needed a ride from work, at the time I didn't know what type of ride I would be giving her. Her car had broken down and she needed a lift home, so I agreed to oblige her. We were riding along making our way to her side of town. She started talking about her boyfriend and how he was treating her, it was bad. I ask her "why do you stay with this guy if he doesn't treat you the way you like to be treated?"

She turn to me and said "I could ask you the same thing", I paused for a second and figured I would come back with a smart reply by saying "to bad we don't just pull this car over and take care of our needs", and she said "why not". I said "What! Are you crazy, your boyfriend is excepting you home and so is my wife". Yes I mean it just like it sounded my wife was expecting her home soon.

Any who she turn to me and said "they'll just have to wait". I'll never forget this little dive of a place was just coming up on our left hand side and I told her if she kept talking like that she was going to make me pull over at the nearest hotel. She said "what's taking you so long".

It just so happen, this dirty little motel was coming up on our left hand side, without blinking I whipped the car around in the middle of the street with tires screeching. I don't think I applied any brakes, I turned into their parking lot, ran up to the night clerk shove some money in his face, grab the keys, grab Gina by the hand and a year later we ended the relationship just barely speaking to each other, what a difference a year makes.

During that year she got rid of her boyfriend at least that's what she told me. She got pregnant and didn't tell me she got rid of the baby. We fell sort of in love, here again I wanted something I wasn't supposed to have so it ended in a disaster.

The real crazy thing is the only people who knew we were dating were the people we told, if my wife suspected me of having an affair she never told me. I ask Givonni, (my wife) some ten years after we were divorced if she knew Gina and I were messing around, she replied, "I often wondered why you were so protective over her during our Aimway trips".

Those Aimway days seem like a million years ago, I wouldn't have the nerve or thoughtlessness today to book a single hotel room (_at least I had sense enough to ask for a room with twin beds_) for both my wife and girlfriend at the same time. My wife and I would be in one bed sleeping while my girlfriend and desires were in the next bed, that's nuts, and totally disrespectful, my head was in a different place then. Aimway got to be a bit much for us, so we quit, but before we did we met a lot of good people trying to make a better life for themselves.

It's a shame how certain groups of people make their money off the desire others have to fulfill their dreams. Thinking people's kindness is a weakness can be a big mistake. The lesson I learned from dealing with Aimway and its philosophy is a lesson all people must learn sooner then later. Everything isn't for everyone and groups like Aimway sell a lot of products, and dreams is their best product.

As my life unfolds onto these pages it's clear to me I was out of touch with reality. I never knew I was such a butt hole until I started writing this book. I don't know why I didn't see myself in the same light as those I hung around. In every city there's a sleazy side of town, and it drew me like a moth to a flame.

I COULDN'T BEGIN TO TELL YOU HOW MUCH MONEY I SPENT ON FAST WOMEN AND SLOW CARS.

CHAPTER 9

FAST WOMEN AND SLOW CARS

I never considered myself as a man who could have any lady friend. As a matter of fact all during high school I wanted nothing to do with girls. To me they were silly and always looking for an opportunity to make you look stupid.

I never played any of the kissing games or hide and go get it. My experiences in life from a young boy into manhood amounted to zero. By the time I join the Navy I was practically a virgin.

The only reason I say almost is because if not for friends asking their girlfriends to open their world to me, my experience prior to joining the service would have been a big zero. Even after I was in the Navy for a while I was very shy and till this day I'm very shy when it comes to women.

One day I saw a friend on his way off base and he asks me if I wanted to go so I said "yes" and off we went. We drove to a strange part of town where these women were just standing on the street looking for something.

He pulls over and whispers something in her ear and she came around to the passenger side of the car and asks me to let her get in. I couldn't even spell the word prostitute let alone know how they work.

She got in and we drove off to this dingy little room, and she got out and told me to follow her. No sooner we got in the room she started taking off her clothes, so I covered my eyes while trying to get a free peek.

She came over to me with just her panties and bra on. To make matters worse, she started trying to take my stuff off too, that wasn't happening. I thought this was a joke my buddy was playing on me so I left the room and went back to the car.

When I got there Wayne asks me if I was finished, I said "finished what?" He said "getting some trim". What the hell was this fool talking about, did I get some trim? I'm pretty damn sure whatever that was I hadn't gotten any. Again he turn to me and said "well", I said "well what." He said "did you have sex with her?"

Now I know he was crazy. How in the hell was I suppose to do any thing like that with a woman I just met, I thought man this guy is going straight to hell.

Not only did I not know this person, I struggled with this act with the girls. I attempted it back home and I grew up with those girls. My Mother had told me on many occasions what the Bible said. So out of respect I said no, I wouldn't try and have sex or anything else with a woman I didn't know, that would be wrong.

I then found out he had paid her ten dollars to break me in. He hollered, "Fool! I paid that ho ten dollars for some pussy for you and you're too stupid to get it".

He used the f word and told me to get my dumb ass in the car; "I'm taking you back to the base"!

On the way back he explained how the system worked, you give a woman of the street money and she give you whatever she might have. For some crazy reason the image of that sweet sister walking up to me in just her under clothes stuck in my head.

After the shock wore off and my hormones started kicking, I ask my friend Wayne could we go back, this time I had my own money. He told me to save my money because a few of the fellas had found this place over in old Mexico where there was nothing but women and they were cheap.

On my first visit I didn't know what to expect. By the time of my second visit I had more money and had changed my mind on soliciting sex, I was hooked. I was developing a habit which would plague me for many years and cost me one marriage, tens of thousand of dollars and almost destroyed my second relationship.

At first it was exciting, a new woman whenever, then I started trying to learn the find art of love making, (screwing). Who better to teach me then the men and women that did it for a profession?

At the age of eighteen I started the fine art of searching the streets for the women of the night. Like everything I do, I jumped into this with both feet.

When I tell you it was exhausting that is an understatement. I learned to prowl the streets until the wee hours of the morning looking for a victim.

I'm not proud of this part of my life, but the name of the book is **This is Your Life,** so I'm sure I'm not the only one. I won't tell the whole story, but I'll say enough to let you know how this thing (**running prostitutes**) got a hold of me.

∽

Just so the audience knows, I got introduced to this sickness at age eighteen and didn't get delivered from it until I was forty five or so years old. I rediscovered God, that's the answer to your question you're asking or at least you should ask.

The question what made me change, and how did I do it, well the answer really is God. Here's how I knew I needed to change the god I was serving. We all have something we serve and what we call it doesn't change the part it plays in our life so I call it a god but not the God.

As I was getting ready to say, my current way of life was starting to weigh heavy on my mind and body, and had just about destroyed my relationship with the one person I really loved.

The reality of just how consumed I was by this life style hit me one morning as I pass by a mirror in the house, I didn't see a reflection. The one person I use to identify with was gone. I backed up to get a better look because this kind of freaked me out, and sure as hell I didn't recognize the person staring back at me.

All I could see was this dark shadow. I stood there for I don't know how long just staring into the mirror. Something my Mother taught me as a little boy, if you find yourself lost, cry out to God and that's just what I did. I just wanted to give some insight on how and why I made a change, through pray and having the best woman in the world (Denise) at my side.

᪐

Now I can tell you how the night life became my life. I didn't know any thing about the under world, but to seek the power I wanted I had to dig deep.

The world of drugs and gambling all leads to prostitutes. Even though I didn't gamble or do drugs at first, I had to deal with the people that lived by taking advantage of others and I had to learn to turn my head and not see the ruthlessness. This way of life became my life so I cared even less then the people that cared nothing at all.

I traveled the back alleys looking for a sex fix never to find anything that even came close. There were times I would spend an entire night looking just for one whore.

Everything about finding a night walker excited me. To know some limp dick fool had her moments before me was part of the game. The choking smell of cheap perfume, the uncertainty in her eyes once you got her in your possession.

How she wore her clothes determine how I treated them, if she was a tramp I had no respect and didn't care how painful it was to her body or mind. I was out to prove a point, that I could take possession of another human being's whole being, and get them to perform for a few dollars.

After a while I learned the game from another perspective, these women needed someone to care for them too, so I change my game plan and learned I didn't have to pay as much or often if I provided some comfort.

So I became some of the night walker's keeper, now ain't that a trip! For you guys reading this don't get it twisted, nothing is free. It's true I didn't spend as much money to be with these women, but it cost me a lot of time and anguish.

Have you ever gotten yourself into something and had a hard time getting out, that's how I feel about this part of the story. The only difference is I have the power of the pen, so I'm bowing out gracefully. So with that being said I believe I've shared all I should about this crazy time in my life, most of you don't believe it anyways. I'll take this as my cue to move on.

So as the writer I'll put pen to paper and continue Denise's story.

CHAPTER 10

THE SAGA CONTINUES

Denise and I lived in her small apartment until we met these people who became the baby sitter for our daughter. The cool thing was they only lived minutes away, just around the corner. This was convenient for us, coincidently; the house next to them was up for sale, so we ended up buying the place.

As our life started looking up, I started having problems over at the other place (Givonni's spot). *Money, money, money, money* that's all people want is *money*.

The life I thought I had left behind was slowly gaining on me, so I had to make some changes. And change I did, first I sat down with Givonni and explain how I was unable to keep up two places.

She complained about me leaving her with all the responsibility. It became obvious to me she was hurt and was using me to keep herself free to party, well that had to come to an end.

By this time a couple of years had slip by so it was time I put my money where my mouth had been, LOL. You know the old saying, it takes two to tango; well it takes two to destroy a marriage.

I just thought I would throw that in here to let the ones among you who are blind know I wasn't alone in this party; it's just I'm the one telling the story to the best of my recollection. There was enough infidelity on both our parts to reserve us a place in hell, is it me or is it starting to get hot in here. In every relationship it becomes easier to blame one another, truth be told, in every case I dealt with, both people were to blame.

Take for an example our marriage, even after Givonni and I decided to move on and go our separate ways, the thought of getting a divorce wasn't part of our plan, that took some seven or eight years later.

Listen to the reason we didn't, Givonni didn't want to be without the title even though she didn't want me and Denise on the other hand wanted me married to protect her from having me fully.

When I ask Denise why she felt this way, she told me she didn't want to be married because she still wanted her freedom. So we went on with this facade, me living with a woman with a daughter that was not mine. And a woman (Givonni) with my last name, but who wasn't mine, what a mess.

Most of you view this whole relationship between Givonni, Denise and me as crazy and chaotic, when in fact if you were to be honest, you couldn't name one relationship that's really good, not perfect but just good and without major problems.

Most of you will never tell your true story to yourself let alone the world, so I'll move on. This whole book has taken on a life of its own, so I find myself reiterating why I started it in the first place.

These are the different paths of my journey through life, which guided me to the love of my life. As this story sways back and forth, the bouts I've had with life's decisions at times has left me on the ground gasping for air. I'm sure you've had similar experiences, but we learn to get up and move back to our corner to come out fighting when the bell sounds, so ding, ding.

CHAPTER 11

TRANSITIONING

In 1990 the company we work for had made too many bad choices and had to lay off ten thousand people, Denise and I were among those numbers. The crazy thoughts that ran through our heads damn near lead us to the end of the cliff, not to jump, but to peek over the edge to see where our future had gone.

I would be lying if I told you it didn't feel like the end of the world because it did. We had been in a major car accident and totally destroyed our car, Denise had gotten pregnant and lost the baby, and Givonni and I were still married. The question was what were we going to do for money? We collected unemployment and also took the money we got for severance pay and decide to build a music studio.

This was a life long dream of mine, to write and play music. I'm not sure why I haven't mentioned this before now, but it's true. I've been a frustrated musician since I was a young boy and as far as I was concern, this lay off was life presenting to me the opportunity to do me.

I already had some equipment I had bought while I was in Italy. It just so happens in my travels I met other musicians with the same desires and they all had some equipment too, so it only made sense to join forces, and BNTB studio was born.

Building this dream was exciting and very hard work. The deal we made was I would foot the bill for the building materials and what ever additional equipment we needed. Then I was to get reimbursed after the studio got up and running, well that never happen. The list of things needed to make a studio grow turned out to cost more than what I expected.

Up to now I had quit a few things, you know weekend projects, other businesses etc. so I didn't want to add not completing the studio to my list. So I poured my heart and money into it. Who just said **OPM (other people money);** in order to use other people money you have to have money. Other wise OPM just becomes a slogan, so if you're broke what do you know.

Somewhere in life we're given this bad advice about how you never use your own money when you want to start a venture. I was taught you have to sacrifice for your dreams, to birth a dream there are some things that need to be in place, I had none. Keep in mind none of us had ever built anything, so this idea of a studio was way beyond our abilities, one of my first mistakes.

We started the construction without plans just a desire to build this thing in my basement, another stupid mistake.

Writing this now is like looking at old fight reels, I can study my mistakes so as not to make them again, but it doesn't stop the pain from the ass whipping I've already gotten. I must say in all fairness to myself I wasn't totally in the blind. I knew I needed to replace the money I was using, so I needed a plan, now here's that plan.

We, meaning my partners and me, discussed ways we could use the studio to replenish or replace the money I agreed on spending. Life's experiences can cost you your life, sorry I digress, remind me later to tell you about carrots, eggs, and coffee.

It's hard for me to relive this part of my life and not sound bitter. Over the years I've tried all types of therapeutic exercises in order to cope with residuals from past mistakes, or life itself. Trying not to become the egg or carrot is the trick.

Here's a good time to point out that when you start anything you must have your own resources, the right people in your corner, opportunities, and a damn good plan. **OPM (other people's money)** now that's a misnomer, no one will invest in you if you haven't invested in yourself.

Here is a truth, it takes money to make money, I often heard this saying, but this one is true. Before I lose one penny on your idea I have to know you've invested enough into your hat you won't quit when times get rough, because they will.

In order, to make my money back first, we came up with this idea. To bring money into our dream we were going to have to develop a customer base and charge them money to use our facility. It's safe to say that never happen, oh we built the studio and it was one of the best of its kind in the area. The part that never materialized was the development of the customer base needed to make back the money it took to build BNTB.

We had people we were working with before the new place. It made sense to use them as a starting base and we did. However, they weren't paying customers, they were projects we were working with and trying to get them record deals. Needless to say the more we learn about our craft the more consumed we got with other projects.

Now I'm not saying I wasn't part of the problem, just like the rest of the guys I loved working in our own place. When you're composing a work of art it helps if you're not stressed for time. That luxury came with a price, before long people were coming to us just to get free studio time. I couldn't afford that, it was costing me money to keep this dream alive.

Not to mention I was reminded that this was the third time I had used my hard earned money to start a business only to lose the money, and the people I started with. As time will tell this was no different.

Denise and I weren't working and I had spent around nine grand on a life long dream and I had no idea how to make it work. Most of you sensible people want to know what I was thinking, brace yourself.

I thought good things came to those who were honest and worked hard. I was taught if you want something and had faith; the something you want would present itself. All my life I was told to work hard for what I wanted and have faith in my works and the rest would take care of itself.

Can you imagine the first time I found this lie out? When you don't have all the ingredients to make something great happen in your life, it's a good possibility that mediocrity will become your closest friend.

I struggled for many of years with this idea that some day my ship would come into port. In a way I guess you could say it did, because I learned a life time lesson, but on the other hand I never seen the damn thing, I always seemed to come up empty handed.

I often reflected back on my life to see if there was anything I could have done differently to change the outcome, I'm still not sure. I was watching a movie one time and it got to a part where this lady was trying to get this young man to see the bright side of life.

He turned to her and said something very profound." **Good things only happen to a few people in the world while bad things happen to us all".** I'm not sure if I buy into that way of thinking, but life has always pointed in that direction for me. Just by writing about these events in my life pisses me off.

They are quiet little reminders of all the things I've tried doing in my early years to propel myself forward in life, only to find out that I got the short end of the stick. The saying "I can do bad by myself", it's true. I never grasped that understanding; I seem to always need some help to do bad!

BNTB consisted of four people, and as far as music was concerned we were second to none. Once we got our sound together it was unique to only our house. So if you wanted a certain sweet R&B blend with a hint of funk topped with hip hop we were the guys to see.

The sound from our studio house became popular in the music world, but we still had one big problem, we didn't know how to transfer this sound in to some real money.

This caused us to fuss and fight a lot of the time. One day this huge cat came to BNTB studio. I heard this light knock and went to answer the door like I've done a thousand times before, but this time it was different.

When I open the door and this is no lie, this dude was so big he blocked the sunlight. When he spoke his voice was soft as cotton, God is funny that way; most people who are large in stature have tiny voices. He asked me if this was BNTB studio; "yeah man come on in, what can I do for you" I asked. It turns out he was working with a group called "***Next Level***".

Just a side note here, these young guys were the best at this game. I soon found out Big C worked with some of the best people in the music business, **whew,** finally someone who could help me make money.

The BNTB crew sat and talked for a couple of hours with Big C, while we listen to the house sound. He turns to me and says "for a bunch of cats working out of the basement, you guys have one of the best sounds around". The fact is, that sound he was referring to took us a year of working for free, until we perfected our skills. He told us he wanted that sound on his next project, and ask, "When could we get started".

Now here's a guy we knew had been places and so his stamp of approval was cool with us. We made arrangements for him to return after May 2, 1992, our target date set for the grand idea we had, "The Show". This show cost us so much money, time and effort just mentioning it makes me tired.

Check out how this crazy idea came into fruition. It started out as a rumor between four guys, you know, just doing some wishful thinking. Then we started talking about how it could be pulled off. Next we started kicking some times frames around. Next came the whammy, we actually psych ourselves into believing we could pull this thing off.

One of the guys in our crew had this brilliant idea. Let me just say to start with we didn't have any money. His proposal was to do a show, not just a show but a show fit for Hollywood. Lights, cameras and action! Now let's roll on. So here's what happen. I don't want you to think I'm being pessimistic when I point out we hadn't made any money and again we were getting ready to get involved in something we had no idea about, now that's just plain stupid.

You would think that would have stopped us, but nooo we "simply" moved forward in spite of ourselves, starting from scratch. This became a way of life for us, so life continued. We decided to find ten unknown artist and make stars out of them and then show them to the world.

I know you may think I'm exaggerating, but I'm not. We had convinced ourselves we could take ten unknowns, add our expertise and make them into stars, whatever that meant. To move the story forward we had three months to reach our goal and I say this with pride we were on time and it was the best show this city had ever seen.

We flew in people from all over the country to see this show; we called *"**The Gala**"*. Our theme was black and gold and it was nothing short of spectacular.

We did this with pocket money, we didn't have any sponsors nor did we charge for the event. Here again we thought if you poured your heart into something and do right by the people, something good would come from it.

Outside of the experience, we did not make one single red penny; in fact we went into debt. And till this day I still feel the pinch from the money I lost some twenty odd years back. Oh I digress, back to the story in how Big C and I hooked up.

As we discussed, he came back a couple months later and laid out his plans for his music project. After entering the studio one morning he no sooner sat down, when he stared for a few seconds then whispered, "man you guys must be making some serious money up in here".

I can tell my response shocked him, "no not really". At first he simply took this as a humble gesture from some modest brothers not wanting to toot their own horn. I assured him that wasn't the case we were telling the truth, he responded by asking "how is that possible?"

Charlie went on to say he could understand if we didn't want to discuss our financial status, but from where he stood or sat, he knew guys with far less talent that was making a killing.

He asked if we would mind him offering some help in that arena and maybe together we could change our position, we said "cool". A few weeks went by Big C had been coming over talking to us and trying to get a clear picture of what our direction was pertaining to the recording industry.

One day the phone rang and it was Charlie on the other line, "hey bro", "yeah what's up" I said. He informed me he wanted to come over to lay some knowledge on me, but this was just for my ears. I said "bring it" and he added, "I may have a proposition for you".

He showed up, and no sooner he entered the room, he started asking what each one of the guys did as far as the studio was concerned. After I explained each person's position, he turns to me and said "hey man you need to get rid of these guys, they're costing you money".

What he said made me sit back in my chair, and out of courtesy I listen to what this brother had to say. At the end of his consultation I knew he was right. One of the last things Big C said to me was, "you can do bad by yourself". My heart was heavy because I knew Charlie had told me the truth, question was what was I going to do about it.

I talked to my life partner (Denise) and we decided to do what was best for the studio. So I had a meeting with the fellas, when I told them what was on my mind they were majorly pissed. Nothing ever goes down just like we say.

The boys and I had many arguments about our present situation; and the thought of me moving on without them had cross my mind several times. I told you I had this thing where I lose people and money. I had already lost the money, I guess the people were next, just kidding, but I told them I would be doing the studio work from now on by myself. However, I didn't tell them I was changing partners. I needed some money, these guys all had some sort of income, where as I was only relying on the money coming into the studio.

I just threw this part in here to let you know I didn't just cold heartily kick my studio buddies out. So every one that was riding my gravy train was shut off, no more free sessions, if you weren't making money you couldn't use the equipment.

Every time Charlie showed up he had money to do his session. This went on until we decide to become full partners. We started a record label **MADD TRAXX Records,** and decided to make breaks and beats.

We looked at the competition, added our twist and within the month we had a product out on the shelf in the record stores. Our first project cost us money, but we both paid for the venture. We sold enough records to break even, so we did another project.

By our second project we had establish our game plan. We didn't have enough money to compete with the other companies doing the same type projects, but we could out class them and that's exactly what we did.

We made our beat unique to our label by just adding a little extra time. Our sounds were cleaner and much easier to use. We sold this product to most rap artist who came through the studio. Everything we did we would try and find a way to make the customer pay for it.

Charlie was true to his word, **BNTB** started making money, but most of the money we made I needed to keep my family living, so the profit margin was really low. It cost no less than six hundred dollars to get a project off the ground and this was in a small way.

To make some real money we needed to up the ante, but here again no capital so our dream started suffering again from lack of life support. Like I said before, it takes money to make money. Charlie and I fought this up hill battle for almost a year.

One day while sitting in the studio a call came through; it was this guy from the country of Australia. He wanted to know how he could get more of our records in his stores in his country. I told Big C about the phone call and he didn't know what the hell was going on.

We soon found out our competition was stealing our material and selling it over seas. There was nothing we could do about it because all this stuff was some what illegal anyways. *Break beats records* use other people's music by sampling a portion of it then taking those pieces and putting them together and making four beat songs. When it came to this Charlie and I were the best.

෴

Since our money was funny, I started toying with the idea of getting a job, what a bitch. So much for freedom, I needed to feed my family. Charlie's wife was having a problem with him spending so much time in our studio, so she started making waves. Pointing out I was keeping the bulk of the money we were making and that he had a job and had to raise two girls. She had good reason to feel this way; the music business itself was like having a mistress. Music does become the other woman, and most men can spend all day every day, in a studio, it's sort of like when they go to the *home improvement store with all those tools.*

Or for the ladies it's like you going to a shoe store and it's a buy one get two for free sale. Charlie did the right thing to listen to his wife even though this would destroy his music endeavors it might save his marriage.

So I started seeing less and less of Charlie until one day I looked up and poof, he was gone. I never heard from him again. Even to this day, I still don't know what happen to him. I was back to square one again like I said before, starting from scratch was a way of life, and here again I met life.

CHAPTER 12

REALITY

Equipment started breaking down with no money to replace it, I needed a job. I remembered running into an old friend some time ago at the **Motors Vehicles Administration** and he was telling me about driving trucks. As a young boy my brother and I would sit in the porch swing all day watching trucks go by.

We always said someday we were going to drive one of those big rigs. Running into Alex must have reignited that childhood dream or maybe I was just desperate.

Either way I found myself taking the test to get my commercial license (CDL). Before the truck thing Denise and I had decided to have a son, give our lives to Christ and get married, but not in that order. By the time I started getting offers from truck companies she was pregnant. I couldn't go over the road so I started driving for a mass transit company.

At first this seemed like a good choice, life was good, I was making a little money, I had a new wife and a new baby boy on the way.

Man I was petrified of that big ass bus and many nights I cried myself to sleep wondering if I had made the right choice.

I had thirty days to learn this new life and two weeks into it I still couldn't drive this damn thing. Most of the time while driving this massive machine my ass would be so tight I couldn't break wind.

Money and choices that's what life boiled down too, whether you have the money to make the right choice or if you make the right choice to have money, either or it's crazy.

My thirty daze were up and I do mean daze not days, the whole time I was learning to control the beast I was in a "daze".

After your initiation they turn you loose on the people, driving while under the influence of fear is more dangerous than any drug.

Weeks went by and before long I was whipping this forty ton monster around the streets of B-More with complete confidence.

Three years came and went and I had taken as much from the public as they could take from me. Dealing with all the drunks and breaking up fights and trying not to get robbed while doing a job got crazy to me. After this young school boy pulled a knife on me and threaten to stab me, I had enough.

The thing that frightened me the most about that day was I was trying to get to my knife first, thank God I had dropped it in another part of the bus earlier without my knowing or I would be writing to you from prison.

This job made you hard, because of all the characters you came in contact with. I was trying to change my life for the good not go back to the mess.

So one sunny day I simply got off the bus never to return. Driving a MTA bus is one job I hope I don't ever have to consider again. Driving has always been a passion of mine, so I continued to drive, from school buses to delivering milk, but what's most important is how each adventure brought me closer to the reason I wrote this book in the first place, the death of Denise.

From the day I first laid eyes on her to the day she transition, she had class. After ten years or so we discovered Denise had diabetes.

Through her whole time dealing with this thief, she never stopped caring for others. Near the end she had started managing gospel groups and like the angle she was she was very good at it.

I watched her put her feelings aside to ensure her people were cared for. If I had to describe Denise I would use a song we both liked very much called "Wildfire". There's a part of the song where it says "she face the hardest time you could imagine but many times her eyes fought back the tears".

If you didn't know Denise you would never know just how sick she was. She could look adversity straight in the eyes and smile. She could take the most unorganized situation and bring order to it, man she had the gift.

Denise so often walked in my shadow not because I was so much of anything; this sister was smart; she knew people feared things they didn't understand. She learn to shield her greatness, she was very modest and most time very shy.

I often wish I had her courage, grace, tenacity and sense of honor. We as humans have a tendency to think we're not perfect but we are, it's just we're perfect in our own unique way.

Remember the song "Wildfire", there's another part of the lyrics that depicts Denise's ability to mask pain. When the song says "and when her useful world was about to fall in, each time her slender shoulders bearing the weight of all her fears, there's a sorrow no one knows, it rings in midnight silence in her ears". The next part of the song I often felt was solely my responsibility, simply put to let her be as free as she could possibly be. Life has a way of preparing us for the inevitable, death, it comes to us all ready or not.

About a year before Denise's death there were many signs pointing to her end. I just didn't have the necessary courage to face the truth like I had promised in our wedding vowels. For better or for worst and to death do us part, remember those words.

They ring in a different key when it's time to hear them again. These words were my sorrow no one heard but me. Like the song says "they ring in midnight silence". So with my heart torn between the belief that her healing was just around the corner, and the cold splash of reality that I was slowly loosing the love of my life, I started to let go.

In a way I died a little each day too, my heart would hurt so bad some days I could do nothing short of dying. To die a slow death behind laughter and a smile made the world happy, but made me more like the egg. I made up every excuse to try and convince myself that death wasn't stalking this beautiful soul, it was in vain, death blew through the window and whisked away her last breath leaving me to pick up the pieces.

∽

Ok this would be a good time to take a break and explain about the reference I've been making about carrots, eggs and coffee. It goes like this, a little girl asked her Mother a question about life and the Mother needing a way to explain to a young mind decided to use objects you can find in some kitchens.

The Mother goes on to enlighten the young person about life by using this example. In life you're going to be put into situations from time to time that may or may not affect your life. If and when that happens she said "I want you to always remember what I'm about to tell you, carrots, eggs, and coffee." "What does this have to do with life" the child asks and the Mother replied.

"Fill these three small pans with water and turn up the fire so the water inside will boil". A few minutes went by and the water started boiling. She instructed the child to place an egg in one pan, coffee in another and carrots in the last one.

Again they waited a few minutes and the Mother said "turn the fire off and let's see how being in hot water changed the items".

After letting each item cool a bit, the Mom removed the egg and placed it in the little girl's hand.

"Do you notice anything different" the Mother asked? "Yes" answered her daughter, the egg got hard enough for me to crack the shell and the insides didn't run out. "Good" replied the Mother, "now what about the carrots?" With a gentle squeeze the carrot smashes in her hand. "What's different about this item she asked?" Well the little girl answered, "It started out hard, but now it's really soft". The girl look at the pan filled with coffee and glared at her Mom and the Mother being wise smiled, "no dear we're going to use two cups for the coffee".

The Mother poured the coffee into the two cups, the Mother motion for the child to sit at the table. "Before we taste this item lets take a moment to smell its aroma", said the Mom. "Umm that smells good" said the daughter; the coffee had turned the water into a brown liquid.

So the Mother said, "What do you see that's different here?" The little girl placed a finger on her temple and looked up into the ceiling and said "the coffee changed the hot water", "very good" exclaimed the Mother!

But the young girl quickly added, "I'm not sure what this all means", "I'm glad you asked that question" the Mother replied. "You see there's going to be many things that may pass your way and will seem like hot water to you, but you don't have to let it make you so hard that life stops flowing from you like the egg. Or it makes you so soft that anyone can squeeze the life out of you like the carrot. The best thing to do is to try and change your surroundings, so you can enjoy its fruit, like the coffee".

When someone we love dies we can allow that death to make us to hard, soft, or we can understand it's just a part of life and enjoy the changes that person brought to the world.

❧

On August, 19th, 2006 a cloud came over me blocking the sun's rays, on December 20th that warm reflected glow turned black, but it was impossible for me to even notice because I was wearing the darkest pair of sun shades known to man.

Who I'm I, the person next door, your friend, a total stranger, but most of all I'm you.

About the Author

W. James Harris, author, philosopher, and motivator has been compiling excerpts of his writings for the last 20 years. His insight into the human psyche is phenomenal. He is a self educated African-American male who was so misunderstood in his childhood that he was believed to be mentally and developmentally challenge. Although Mr. Harris never completed his formal education, he spent many years studying psychology and the teachings of some of the great philosophers such as Frantz Fanon, Aldous Huxley and Frances Cress Welsing. His mind has a way of thinking which has no limits. He has an uncanny ability to conceptualize and dissect the minuscule to the most intense thought or school of thought. The norm does not exist for this man, he has no boundaries. Taping into God's infinite wisdom has always been his goal and his desire. This journey we call life has always been intriguing to him and he has spent his life exploring the vast possibilities it can bring. As people he believes we have limited ourselves in our thinking, our understanding and striving to be all that we were created to be. The expedition that you're about to walk through is an Arduous Journey through the depths of "Your Life and Your Mind" with Mr. Harris as your guide.